ISBN: 979-8-9991260-3-0
Library of Congress Control Number: 2026900093

# About the Author

Before internet, cellphones, social media and computers, Jareth Bramblewick grew up wandering the piney woods and creeks of North Florida, where quiet afternoons and curious creatures first sparked his imagination. Eventually, his journey carried him far from the warm, wild backcountry to the rocky coast of Camden, Maine, a place that stole his heart with its salty sea breeze, mossy forests, and working harbor boats.

In Camden, Jareth found a rhythm of life that echoed with wonder. He explored the whispering waters of the Megunticook River, played ice golf across Chickawaukie Pond, and rode the ferry from Rockland to North Haven and Vinalhaven, where spruce scented air met the open sea. It was here, along Maine's misty shores and shadowed woodland paths, that his love for nature deepened and bloomed into story.

Exploring gratitude, impermanence, and the quiet wonder of everyday life. Living along the coast where mountains meet the sea, he draws inspiration from morning walks through Camden Harbor, the changing light over Megunticook Lake, and the hush of winter fog rolling in from Penobscot Bay.

His reflections blend nature, memory, and philosophy into lyrical narratives that celebrate both solitude and connection. When he's not writing, Bramblewick can often be found wandering coastal trails, sketching story ideas by the water, or gathering inspiration for the next chapter of his Maine seasons series.

For one year, the author walked the back roads, shoreline paths, and quiet trails between two Maine harbor towns. What began as simple wandering became something deeper, an unfolding conversation between place and thought. Camden and Rockport reveal themselves slowly, through winter snow settling over empty paths, spring lupine rising along stone walls, and harbor light that softens even the busiest mind.

This book is not a guide, nor a memoir in the traditional sense. It is a collection of meandering reflections shaped by movement, stillness, and the gentle influence of land and water. In the calm of these towns, the author discovers a quieter interior landscape, one shaped by patience, memory, and the freedom to think without urgency.

Between Harbor and Pine is an invitation to slow down, to take the long way, and to experience Maine not as a destination, but as a state of mind.

# Years on the Road

I have been moving for most of my life. Fifteen years around America. Thirty if you count the years I wandered the world before that. Sometimes I think movement became my closest companion. Sometimes it felt like escape.

Germany was the first real chapter. I was in my early twenties, not old enough to understand how rare those years would be. I worked hard, spent too much time thinking there would always be another weekend to explore, another train to catch. I did travel some, Nuremberg, Rothenburg, the small towns stitched between the rivers, but I see now how much more I could have seen if I'd understood that time only runs one way. Germany was beautiful. It still lives somewhere inside me, the sound of church bells, the heavy air before rain, the smell of bread from a corner bakery I never learned the name of.

Then came Hawaii. That place changed me. Work is a blur now, but I remember the evenings, the North Shore, the sunsets that burned and then vanished, eating ice cream at the Dole plantation with my son, the movie on the beach in Waikiki with him and my mother when she came to visit. I remember laughter, sand on our clothes, the way night fell without warning. Hawaii taught me what ease felt like, even if only for a short time.

Later, Okinawa. The air there carried salt and history. It was a place that seemed both alive and haunted, quiet and deep. My son was still young enough to see everything as new, and through him I saw it too, the markets, the temples, the sea walls, the soft order of daily life. That place taught me reverence.

When I came back to the States, I took a contract in Portland, Oregon. January. I arrived with one suitcase and no car. I walked to work through snow that rose to my knees. When spring came, I bought a bicycle and never stopped using it. I rode to work, through cherry blossoms, across bridges, along the river. I learned the city by the turn of its trails. I remember hearing Burn by Ellie Goulding for the first time there. That song still smells like wet pavement and cold air and freedom.

Then New Mexico. I thought it would be nothing but desert. I was wrong. I stayed a year in a hotel room because there were no rentals, but the landscape made up for it. The light was unreal. The skies seemed to go on forever. I remember a winter trip with my son to a roadside hot spring near Las Vegas, New Mexico. Snow all around. Steam rising from the water. We slipped into the heat and laughed at how it almost burned. We found a rhythm, hot spring to frozen river, back again, until the air stung and our skin glowed red. It felt like being alive in a way that made you forget everything else.

The Carolinas came next. Work again, and the quiet beauty of the Blue Ridge, the long rolling hills, the slow fade of evening light. I carried the same pattern everywhere, work, walk, notice, remember. The world kept changing, but something inside me began to settle.

And then Maine.

I didn't expect Maine to feel the way it does. The first breath of ocean air here felt like a reset. Cold, clean, briny. Everything smells alive. The water along the coast is so clear it feels wrong to call it water, it's something sharper, something that cuts and heals at the same time.

The peace here is unlike anywhere else I've been. Even the small things surprise me. People leave their car windows open when they go shopping. You can walk for hours and not hear a siren. There's an honesty in that kind of safety.

Now I spend my evenings walking. Camden to Rockport, the same 5.8 mile loop, sometimes in silence, sometimes with thoughts that drift in and out like the tide. The mountains rise behind me, Mount Battie, Beech Hill. I take the harder trails on purpose, even when I know there's an easier one. Something in me prefers the climb.

When I reach the top, I look out over the harbors and the cold Atlantic beyond them. I think of every place I've been. I think of how each one left something in me that the next never erased.

There's no lesson in it. Just the sound of the wind. Just a man walking another stretch of his life, remembering the roads behind him and the quiet that keeps him company now.

# The Left Turn, Evening Soliloquy

I've been here a year now. Long enough for the roads to remember my footsteps. Rain, snow, or sun, it doesn't matter. After work, I walk. Always the same route. The short 5.8 miles curling from Camden to Rockport and back again, around Beauchamp Point where the ocean breathes against stone.

It's the hour between worlds, quitting time. The steady parade of cars passing by, the rhythm of headlights and tired faces, people heading home, maybe late for dinner, maybe thinking of nothing at all. Some drive out here on purpose, park by the Children's Chapel, and sit in their cars for a few minutes before walking down to the water. You can tell when someone just needs quiet.

The air smells like pine and briny salt.

But recently I've found something new. A left turn near the cemetery. Small road, tucked away, like a secret. If I take it, no matter the hour, 4:30, 5:30, 6, even closer to seven, it's empty. I mean completely still. No cars. No sound but the wind and the tide.

At first, I thought it was coincidence. Then I started to notice the houses there. Massive places, set back from the road, glass and granite and quiet money. Homes that look out over the ocean, some east, some northeast, each one catching the light differently. From the road, you can see the sweep of porches, the dark silhouettes of decks where maybe someone stands at dusk, wine in hand, watching the tide roll in.

I've come to realize the people here live by a different clock. They aren't hurrying home from work. They're already there. Maybe they've been there all day. Maybe they never needed to work in the way the rest of us do.

It's strange, walking past their driveways. The air feels heavier somehow. Not threatening, just... removed. A kind of stillness money can buy. A life that doesn't rush or scrape or bargain with time.

Once, I paddled along the coast from Camden, just to see it from a distance, from the water. The houses rising from the rocks, all glass and cedar, set against the trees. The sea lapping against private coves I'll never step onto. It was beautiful in a distant way, like looking into another world from behind a pane of glass.

And yet, I still take that left turn. I like its silence. Its emptiness. I don't envy those homes anymore. I just want to understand what it feels like to be still. To have a life so unhurried that you forget what quitting time means.

So I keep walking. Past the chapel, the headstones, the curve of the shore. Watching the light change over the water. Thinking, not thinking.

Just walking.

# Gyoji: A New Life on the Coast

There is a word from Japan, Gyoji. **The practice that perpetuates itself**. Not something you pick up for a week and set down again. Not another half-finished attempt at change. It is the act of remaking a life, and refusing to let it slip.

For years I lived like a tide that never quite knew where it was heading. I would start something, a notebook, a routine, a promise to myself, and let it scatter when the first storm of distraction came. I blamed exhaustion or circumstance. But the truth was inside me, a small, sly voice that whispered every morning.

Should I rise now, or stay warm beneath the blankets? Should I write, or leave it for tomorrow? Should I walk the shore, or pour another cup of coffee and drift?

Those negotiations were constant. They wore me down. They gave me permission to quit, over and over again. And each time I quit, the voice grew stronger.

But there came a day when I decided the old self had to die. Not in violence, but in refusal. I would no longer bargain with myself. I would no longer let the voice run my life.

So I built a schedule as firm as the harbor's granite breakwater. I rose at the same hour, before dawn, no matter what. I sat on the floor and let the breath steady me. Meditation. Non negotiable. I stretched into yoga until the muscles learned the posture before the mind had a chance to resist. Then I walked outside, cold salt air on my face, and I watched the sunrise over Camden Harbor, the masts catching fire in that early light. And then I wrote. A page at first. Then three. Then a chapter. Now it is simply what I do, as fixed as the tide.

There are days when the old voice tries to return. Shouldn't you rest? Haven't you earned a break? What harm could it do to skip just this once? I know those words. I know the trap. But now the practice answers for me.

Gyoji.

The word itself becomes a shield. The body rises while the mind resists. The hand reaches for the pen. The breath steadies itself. The practice perpetuates the practice. There is no argument anymore, because the schedule is already set, and the habits are no longer negotiable.

Here on the coast of Maine, where gulls circle above the tide and woodsmoke drifts in the evening air, I live as a different person. The one who hesitated, who drifted, who bargained away his mornings, is gone. In his place stands someone else. Stronger and more steady.

A life made of practice. A life that carries itself forward.

Gyoji.

# The Secret of Camden and Rockport

As summer bows and autumn takes the stage, Camden and Rockport breathe with quiet grace. The harbors soften, sails are furled, and the tide hums its ancient song. The tourists drift away, but the towns do not fall silent, instead, they settle into their truest selves.

Leaves ignite in bursts of gold and crimson, spinning like confetti across winding streets, as if the sea itself has tossed them into the air. Woodsmoke drifts from chimneys and mingles with the salt breeze, carrying with it a hush of memory. Each evening grows crisp, each morning sharp with light, and still the boats rest gently in their moorings, captains folding lines with practiced hands.

It is a season of secrets. Camden whispers them through rustling birches, Rockport sighs them across its quiet docks. To linger here is to feel the gift of impermanence, to know that beauty is fleeting, yet more precious because of it. A little breeze carries this truth along, weaving through golden days and silvered nights, reminding all who pass that every ending carries within it the beginning of another.

And so these two coastal towns stand together, tender, timeless, and true. For those who wander here, the memory does not fade. It settles into the heart like saudade, that longing for what is already slipping away, even as it surrounds you still. Camden and Rockport keep their secret well, yet share it freely with anyone who pauses long enough to listen.

Camden Harbor

# Staying Still

I never thought I'd stay anywhere this long. A year, maybe two at most. But Maine has a way of holding you. Not with grand gestures, not with anything loud. It keeps you through silence, through repetition. Through the kind of peace that feels almost unearned.

For so many years, I measured life in departures. New assignments, new places, new rooms that never quite became home. I had learned how to leave without thinking twice. But here, I find myself staying.

At first, it felt strange. I would wake early and feel that old pull, the urge to move, to plan, to go somewhere. But the harbor outside my window would stop me. The stillness of it. Boats waiting in the morning fog. The faint sound of gulls in the distance. The quiet rhythm of a place that doesn't care whether you hurry.

I started walking again. Every evening, the same loop. Camden to Rockport. Then back. The road taught me that change can happen even when nothing looks different. The same corners, the same pine trees leaning toward the water, the same air, cold, clean, alive. But each day, something shifts inside me.

Sometimes I think about what it means to stay put. Not just in geography, but in the body, in the mind. I spent half my life chasing something I couldn't name. Maybe it was freedom. Maybe distraction. Here, I don't chase anything. I let the world come to me.

I notice the sound of gravel underfoot when the road is dry. The way the ocean smells sharper in late afternoon. The porch light at the old house near the curve that always turns on too early. These are small things, but they root me.

There are evenings when fog settles so thick that I can't see ten feet ahead. I keep walking anyway. The sound of my own breath becomes enough.

Sometimes I stop at Beauchamp Point and watch the tide pull itself away from the rocks, leaving seaweed glistening in the dim light. The wind carries salt and something else I can't quite name, something that reminds me I'm still here, still learning how to be still.

I've met a few people along this road. Not many. A nod, a soft hello. Most of them seem to walk for the same reason I do, to quiet the noise inside. There's comfort in that, even without words.

It's strange how staying can feel like a form of travel. The landscape outside doesn't move, but something inside keeps unfolding, mile after mile, evening after evening.

When I reach the end of my walk, the light is usually fading. I pause before going inside, looking out toward the water. There's no rush to end the day. The air tastes of salt and pine. The world feels patient.

I used to think motion was what made a life. Now I think it's attention. The willingness to look closely. The willingness to stay.

And so I do.

# Sanctuary Between Two Harbors

It has been a year since I started walking the long loop from Camden to Rockport. What began as a way to clear my head after work has become a kind of ritual. I walk it in all weather, rain, snow, the bright haze of summer. Sometimes the wind comes in strong off the water and I have to lean against it just to keep moving, but I always go.

Over time, the road has become a part of me. I know where the pavement dips, where the smell of seaweed rises, where the gravel shifts underfoot. What surprises me is how much more I see now than when I first began.

It started with small things. A cluster of plants I had never noticed before. A fox crossing the road at dusk. The way the light changes color along the shore as the sun lowers behind Mount Battie. There's no rush, no checklist. I just walk and notice. Each day offers something new, something simple.

The more I pay attention, the more I want to. There's a quiet fullness in it.
Lately, I think about my father when I walk. The way he used to stand in the yard in the evenings, watching the light fade, hands in his pockets, not saying much. I remember the steadiness of him, the kind of patience that comes only from living long enough to understand that most things don't need to be hurried. I used to see that stillness as passivity. Now I think it was peace.

I wonder how my son is doing. We talk less than we should. Life gets filled with things that feel urgent until they aren't. I catch myself thinking of what I'd tell him about these walks, the air here, the sound of the tide at night, the value of quiet repetition. How some of the best parts of life are the moments no one else sees.

The road has become a kind of teacher. It doesn't ask for much. Just time. Just attention.

There are stretches where I don't pass a single car for half an hour. Sometimes a local jogger waves or a couple walks by with a dog, but most evenings it's just me. The absence of conversation doesn't feel lonely anymore. It feels like a pause I needed but never knew how to ask for.

Somewhere along this path between Camden and Rockport, I found a place that feels outside the rest of the world. A small borderland between movement and stillness. The rhythm of walking becomes a kind of meditation, step, breath, step. Thoughts rise and fall like the tide.

I don't expect revelation. I don't expect answers. But I find that the longer I walk, the more I begin to trust the quiet. The world narrows down to what's in front of me, the sound of my boots, the smell of pine, the call of a distant gull.

When I return home, the noise of the day still exists, but it doesn't touch me the same way. Something about the road, its length, its solitude, its persistence, seems to rinse the mind clean.

This stretch of Maine coast, between Camden and Rockport, has become more than a route. It's a sanctuary. A place where I remember how to be present. A place that keeps teaching me how little I need to feel whole.

I don't know how long I'll live here, or how many more seasons I'll walk this road. But I know this: when I'm out there, the rest of life feels quieter, lighter, more possible.

And so, every evening, I lace up my boots and go.

Just to walk.

# The Quiet Season

It's been another winter on the coast, long and gray and bone-deep. The kind that seeps into you. The kind that makes silence louder.

I kept walking anyway. Every day, every evening, through snow thick enough to swallow sound. The road around Beauchamp Point became a line I traced again and again, like writing the same word until it starts to mean something else.

Now the ice is gone. The salt air is soft again. The gulls are louder. The sun sets later.

Camden feels alive, like someone slowly waking from a dream. There's that same left turn near the cemetery. The same quiet road. But it feels different now. Not because of what's changed around me, but because of what's changed inside.

I used to walk and wonder about the people in those homes, how they lived, what it must feel like to never rush. I imagined the slow breakfasts, the fireplaces, the lives that looked settled. But now, I hardly think of them.

The envy has faded into something else. Curiosity maybe, or acceptance. I've realized that peace isn't owned. It's practiced. You can have everything and still fidget through the hours, or you can have almost nothing and walk the same road every day and feel full.

The truth is, I like my own repetition. It's its own kind of wealth. Each evening, I see the same pines bending toward the sea, the same chipped guardrail, the same porch lights flickering on one by one.

And somehow it never feels exactly the same. The tide changes, the clouds shift, the air smells different.

Sometimes, in the colder months, I'd see my breath floating in front of me and imagine it carrying all the noise of my day out into the air, gone before it even reached the treetops.

There's a peace in that. A small forgetting.

I think often about what it means to stay. Not just in one place, but in one practice.

To do something every day without needing it to lead somewhere. The road itself becomes the prayer.

Now, when I pass the chapel or the headstones or the curve where the water flashes silver, I don't need anything from the walk. I just move through it, and it moves through me.

Sometimes I still look at the houses on that left turn, the big windows, the terraces facing the ocean. But I don't wonder about the people inside anymore. I just imagine the light spilling out of their rooms, crossing the cold water, touching the rocks, the trees, me.

And then I keep walking.

Always walking.

# Nostalgic Campfire Story

You know, sitting here by the fire, with the sparks rising like small prayers, I'm remembering those morning walks up in Maine. Beauchamp Point, right at the curve where you see the bay stretching open, that's where it started for me.

I used to walk those roads every morning. Quiet, mist rising off the water, smell of pine needles crushed underfoot. And the people, you'd see them, sure, but they'd pass like ghosts. Eyes locked on a phone, or somewhere far away in thought.

So I tried something. Nothing big. I just said Hi. Sometimes Good Morning. And the funny thing is, it felt almost radical, like knocking on a stranger's door. Some folks startled, some barely answered, but a few... a few lit up, like I'd given them something they didn't know they needed.

It wasn't only Camden or Rockport. I noticed the same everywhere, cities and towns, north and south. We've forgotten the ritual of greeting. Forgotten how a word can tilt a whole day in a new direction.

I don't know why I'm telling you this now, maybe because the firelight makes me think of all the mornings I never wrote down, never saved. Maybe because I want to remember that even the smallest words can travel further than you'd expect.

And that's all. Just Hi.

# Beauchamp Point, early morning walk

The bay was silver today, a thin mist curling up from the water. I walked the road the way I always do, slow, just to hear the gravel give under my shoes.

What strikes me most, and not only here in Camden or Rockport, is the quiet between people. You pass them, dog leash in one hand, phone in the other, and it's as if we've all agreed not to look up. Not to greet.

I've started saying Hi anyway. Sometimes Good Morning. Sometimes nothing more than a nod. It feels like dropping a pebble in still water. Small ripples, but real.

Some people look startled, as if I pulled them out of a dream. Others smile, almost shy, like they'd been waiting for permission. And a few don't answer at all, though even then, I imagine the word trailing after them, hovering, maybe catching up later when they least expect it.

I've seen this everywhere, cities that never sleep, little towns with only one store, roads in the middle of nowhere. Silence growing heavier, heads bent toward glowing screens.

So I keep writing this down, or telling it when the fire is low and the night is open. A reminder to myself as much as to anyone listening: the simplest word can change the shape of a day.

Hi. That's all. Hi.

# A Year of Gratitude on the Maine Coast

When I first arrived in Maine, it was November. The air had already turned sharp and heavy with salt, and the harbors lay still beneath a quilt of fog and wind. The docks were empty, the boats pulled ashore, their hulls wrapped in white plastic like cocoons waiting for spring. It feltlike arriving at the end of something.

But endings, I would learn, have their own kind of beginning.

The days grew shorter. Nights stretched out, cold and starless. I lit candles in the evenings, wrapped myself in blankets, and found warmth in small rituals, a steaming cup of tea, a wool sweater pulled from the line, the creak of the old floorboards beneath my feet. Even in the depths of winter, I could smell the sea, faint and briny, like a ghost of summer carried on the wind. That scent reminded me that the ocean was never far, even when hidden beneath ice.

It was then I discovered Hygge, the Danish word that captures a kind of quiet joy born from simplicity and closeness. It became my compass through winter, light the fire, be still, give thanks.

Gratitude started to mean something different to me. It wasn't about having more anymore, it was about seeing what was already right in front of me. The wind against the windows reminded me that warmth was a gift. And the deep, echoing quiet of a snow covered morning reminded me that even stillness has its own kind of life.

By late spring, the transformation was everywhere. The harbors came back to life almost overnight, men and women hauling out mooring lines, the thud of boots on wooden docks, laughter echoing over the cold harbor. Boats bobbed again in the current. Sailboats, lobster boats, kayaks, the coast awakening from its long sleep. The air grew warmer, and the briny scent returned, fuller now, alive with sunlight and seaweed and salt.

Then came summer, and with it, color. Lawns erupted in blossoms I couldn't name, lupines, wild roses and bergamot, growing thick along the roadside. The fields shimmered green under endless blue skies. Evenings stretched late into golden hours, the air soft and smelling faintly of pine and briny ocean spray. I thought of Florida then, the place I'd come from, all heat and sameness, and how here, every day felt like a page turning.

The locals jokingly complained when the temperature climbed into the eighties. I smiled quietly, remembering summers that never dipped below ninety-five. Gratitude again, in a different form, for cool air, for the laughter of neighbors, for ice cream dripping down my wrist in the sun.

And then, like clockwork, autumn arrived.

The shift was instant, almost ceremonial. The air sharpened, the maples began to burn red and gold, and once again, the harbors filled with movement, this time in reverse. Boats hoisted out, shrink wrap pulled tight, docks lifted and stacked. Conversations lingered longer; everyone seemed to say goodbye to summer and to the rhythm that had carried us all year.

Jocularly, some said it was a sad time. And yet, I found peace in it.

Because I understood now, the beauty of this place wasn't just in its color or its calm, but in its impermanence.

Winter came again. I watched the first snow fall on the same docks I'd seen bare a year before. The briny wind returned, faint but unmistakable, threading through the cold like a memory. I made a small fire, brewed tea, and smiled.

For the seasons that passed like breath.
For the people and places that change and return.
For the chance to be still long enough to notice it all.

# The Harbors of Impermanence

In Camden Harbor, in Rockport's tide,
 time lingers like a lantern flame,
 fragile, flickering, impossibly bright.
 Each sailboat leans into its mooring
 as if listening to the whispers of the sea,
 and I walk the summer streets
 already haunted by autumn's breath.

This is anticipatory nostalgia,
 the ache of missing what I still hold,
 the sadness stitched into joy,
 as though the present were already memory.
 It is the weight of impermanence,
 the truth that beauty carries its ending
 even as it blooms.

There is something here,
 The laughter soft as water against the rocks,
 the presence both anchor and horizon.
 I keep my distance,
 yet every step closer is a sweetness
 I know will turn forlorn
 when distance and time claim her.

And yet I cannot help but feel saudade,
 that longing for what is still near,
 that tender sorrow that glows brighter
 the harder I try to resist.

It is the same sadness in the falling leaf,
  the same radiance in a fleeting sunset:
  an awareness of impermanence
  that brings both beauty and sadness.

To love this harbor, this moment, this wonderful moment
in time is to grieve them even while they are mine.
  And perhaps that is the purest form of love:
  to let the heart break wide open
  not in farewell,
  but in the very midst of holding.

# Cloudy With a Chance of Inner Peace

I used to chase the sun like it owed me something. Give me heat, give me light, give me sweat rolling down my back like nature's applause. Summer meant joy. Or at least that's what I was told.

But somewhere along the winding trail of adulthood, something shifted. Now? Now I wake up to a gray sky and think, "Ah, finally, the world has matched my favorite hoodie."

The chill in the air doesn't bother me. It sharpens things. Clears the static. Makes a warm drink feel like a reward and not a survival tactic. The overcast sky wraps around me like a blanket that doesn't expect anything in return. No blinding optimism. No vitamin D pressure.

People talk about seasonal depression when the clouds roll in, but for me? The gloom brings a strange kind of joy. A cozy melancholy. A day where the weather says, "Don't rush. Just…exist."

Maybe it's age. Maybe it's wisdom. Or maybe I'm just turning into one of those moody background characters in an indie film who stares out the window and says things like, "I like the rain. It drowns out the noise."

Whatever it is, give me the cool days. The misty mornings. The kind of weather that makes soup feel spiritual. Let the world have its endless summers, I'll be over here, quietly thriving under a blanket of clouds, sipping something warm and pretending I'm in a Wes Anderson montage.

# Humuhumunukunukuapua'a

Beneath the bright reef, a parrot fish drifted through turquoise light, puffing tiny clouds of sand with every nibble. He fancied himself the painter of the sea, scattering color wherever his teeth met coral. He bragged to the shrimp and sea cucumbers, boasting that his scales caught the sun better than any pearl. But that pride began to wobble the day a Humuhumunukunukuapua'a floated into his corner of the reef, a name that twisted the tongue and a presence that twisted the parrot fish's confidence.

The newcomer moved with swagger, a patchwork of stripes and snout and rhythm. When he grinned, the whole lagoon seemed to laugh. The parrot fish tried to keep up, circling and darting, spouting lines about being "king of the coral," but the Humuhumu only winked and said, "Talk is cheap, friend. Show me your swim." They spiraled together through a cloud of bubbles, neither winning, both forgetting what they were fighting for.

When the sun fell lower, the reef turned quiet. The parrot fish hovered beside the Humuhumu, both of them breathing in the slow pulse of the tide. There was no more boasting. Just two creatures, vivid and ridiculous, sharing the sea that didn't care who shined brighter. The ocean rolled on, the coral shimmered softly, and the laughter of their earlier duel lingered like a song still rippling through the water, one that only the waves remembered the words to.

# Where the Meadow Breaths

Out in the quiet folds of the countryside, the world hums soft and slow. A squirrel darts along a maple branch, its tail flicking like a banner in the sun, while nearby a butterfly drifts through the air, weightless, almost thoughtless, as if it were a dream that forgot to end. The two cross paths beneath a sky that smells faintly of hay and open fields. Their lives could not be more different, yet here they are, sharing the same rhythm of daylight and wind.

The squirrel busies himself with the work of tomorrow, stashing away what the earth provides. He knows the cold will come. The butterfly, though, she seems to know only now. Her wings catch the light like small stained glass windows, fragile but eternal in their moment. He watches her and feels a curious ache, one he doesn't understand. Maybe it's envy. Maybe it's wonder.

Somewhere between them, the meadow holds its breath. The air thickens with the hum of bees and the low murmur of summer's end. The squirrel pauses in his gathering. The butterfly hovers above a clover bloom. Time stretches and folds, and for a brief heartbeat, it feels like the world is whole, no rush, no reason, no regret.

And then, as all things must, the moment drifts. The butterfly lifts toward the horizon, wings fading into gold. The squirrel returns to his work. Life continues, as it always does, in the quiet grace of small things, a lesson written in fur and wingbeats, beneath a country sky that has seen it all before.

Then came summer, and with it, color. Lawns erupted in blossoms I couldn't name, lupines, wild roses and bergamot, growing thick along the roadside. The fields shimmered green under endless blue skies. Evenings stretched late into golden hours, the air soft and smelling faintly of pine and briny ocean spray. I thought of Florida then, the place I'd come from, all heat and sameness, and how here, every day felt like a page turning.

The locals jokingly complained when the temperature climbed into the eighties. I smiled quietly, remembering summers that never dipped below ninety-five. Gratitude again, in a different form, for cool air, for the laughter of neighbors, for ice cream dripping down my wrist in the sun.

And then, like clockwork, autumn arrived.

The shift was instant, almost ceremonial. The air sharpened, the maples began to burn red and gold, and once again, the harbors filled with movement, this time in reverse. Boats hoisted out, shrink wrap pulled tight, docks lifted and stacked. Conversations lingered longer; everyone seemed to say goodbye to summer and to the rhythm that had carried us all year.

Jocularly, some said it was a sad time. And yet, I found peace in it. Because I understood now, the beauty of this place wasn't just in its color or its calm, but in its impermanence.

Winter came again. I watched the first snow fall on the same docks

I'd seen bare a year before. The briny wind returned, faint but unmistakable, threading through the cold like a memory. I made a small fire, brewed tea, and smiled.

For the seasons that passed like breath.
For the people and places that change and return.
For the chance to be still long enough to notice it all.

The snowy season is just beginning here in Camden and Rockport. The first flakes were soft and shy, drifting down only to vanish as quickly as they came. Nights linger near freezing, and days rise just enough for the roads to breathe again. My time in these harbor towns is closing now, late November, the turning of the year, the quiet shift before winter settles in for good. I never imagined this place would hold so much beauty or stir something so deep in me.

Leaving carries a heaviness I didn't expect. The people here have been kind in ways that stay with you. My coworkers have felt more like steady companions than colleagues. The trails around the hills and ponds, the scent of salt in the wind, the steady pulse of the tides, none of it fades just because I'm packing my bags. I drove through Camden and Rockport this morning for one last look, and the whole landscape felt like it was offering a soft farewell. This place doesn't just look cinematic; it feels like a world someone would write about to remind others that quiet wonders still exist.

Now I'm heading south again, back to Florida, where the warmth never hesitates and the summers carry a weight Maine never does. I already feel the contrast pressing in, and part of me wants to hold on to this northern calm a little longer.

I don't want to leave, yet I know I have to. A new chapter waits, career shifts, life changes, the slow approach of retirement. Everything is shifting at once, folding into whatever comes next. Leaving Maine feels like closing a well loved book, but I carry the story with me as I step toward the next one.

# What the Dogs Accidentally Taught Me About People

I finally made the long migration back home, with Camden and Rockport, Maine behind me, Florida once again under my feet. And I'll admit it right away: I miss those evening walks. I miss them more than I expected.

Back in Camden, walking felt almost ceremonial. Quiet streets. Soft light. People who nodded hello. Dogs existed there too, of course, but they behaved like they'd read the rulebook. Leashed, calm, friendly. One neighbor's dog never even crossed the invisible border of its own yard, as if the grass line were a sacred boundary agreed upon by dog and universe alike. I never worried. I never armed myself with bear spray. No taser. No ultrasonic gadget that sounds like a UFO arguing with a dolphin. Just me, the sidewalk, and the strange luxury of peace.

Those neighborhoods, yes, expensive ones, the kind with price tags that could make a mortgage faint, had something else going for them. Courtesy. Not the forced kind, not the performative politeness, but the quiet understanding that other humans exist and deserve space. I've seen friendly places before. I've seen polite places. But that level of mutual consideration? Rare.

Now I'm back where I grew up, in one of the poorest counties in Florida. I still have a foothold here, but each time I travel and then return, the contrast hits harder. It makes my mind wander in uncomfortable directions. How can people be so different within the same country? Same laws. Same flag. Entirely different social contracts.

My first walk back home answered that question swiftly. Three dogs chased me. Not jogged alongside. Not wagged hello. Chased. I stood my ground, deployed pepper spray into the air, activated the ultrasonic repelling device, and reminded myself that this is apparently what morning cardio looks like now.

The next day, I tried a new route. That hope, was a mistake. Two more dogs burst out of their owners yards and surrounded me in the road, circling, barking, close enough to make every instinct scream. I've been attacked by a "friendly" dog before, so I don't gamble on optimism anymore.

An owner finally appeared. I yelled, because between barking dogs and basic survival, volume felt appropriate, and asked her to get her dogs under control. She laughed. Laughed. Repeatedly informed me that the dogs were "in her yard," despite the fact that we were all very clearly standing in the road, having a confrontation that no one had agreed to attend. She told me to "just keep walking." I explained, again loudly, that I couldn't, because her dogs were running at me blocking the way and auditioning for a horror film.

Eventually, they backed off enough for me to retreat, walking backward like a man negotiating a ceasefire with gravity itself.

This is my daily reality now. Dogs everywhere. Running loose. Chasing. Barking without warning. And every morning, like clockwork, they decorate my yard with what can only be described as aggressively confident piles of feces. No apologies. No owners in sight. Just the scent of evidence brewing in the Florida sunshine.

So I find myself thinking about the mentality behind it all. The difference isn't money alone. It's not education in the academic sense. It's the idea of responsibility, to neighbors, to strangers, to the shared space between us. In one place, people seem to think, "How do my actions affect others?" In another, the question never arrives.

I can analyze it philosophically. I can try to understand it sociologically. But I still carry bear spray on my walks now, and that detail alone tells the story better than any theory ever could.

Discover More by J. Bramblewick


The adventures don't end here...

Explore more stories that bring the magic of
Maine's harbors, lakes, and woodlands to life.


Look for more books to come in the future!


Find J. Bramblewick's books in your local
bookstore and explore videos of the real places
that inspired these tales on You Tube.


Keep exploring. Keep imagining. Keep reading.

A year spent walking between Camden and Rockport altered me in ways I did not anticipate. The steady presence of the harbors, the unhurried streets, the back roads threading through pine and weathered stone, all worked quietly on my thoughts.

In that calm, my mind began to wander more freely, no longer pushed by urgency but guided by stillness. The beauty here is not loud, it arrives slowly, through winter light on snow, spring flowers along a forgotten path, and the patient rhythm of the water. That gentleness opened places within me I had not visited before, spaces shaped by reflection rather than motion.

I understand now why people are drawn to Maine, not simply for what it shows the eye, but for how it invites the soul to settle, to listen, and to remember itself.

www.ingramcontent.com/pod-product-compliance
Lightning Source LLC
Chambersburg PA
CBHW042034120726
47911CB00027B/739